STAR
THE
CLONE
WARS

CONTENTS

£7.99

PROFILES

Master Yoda

➔ As the oldest member of the Jedi Council, Yoda's wisdom and strength in the Force are invaluable. He is gentle and kind, with an impish sense of humour. However, he is also a skilled warrior and an astute general.

Master Obi-Wan Kenobi

➔ Over the course of the Clone Wars, Obi-Wan has grown in wisdom and ability. He has become a highly respected member of the Jedi Council, and his good sense and fairness have made him many friends.

Ahsoka Tano

➔ The Togrutan Padawan, nicknamed Snips by her Master, is an independent and gifted Jedi. Her intelligence and skills make her the ideal companion for Anakin Skywalker, but will she also develop some of his more disobedient qualities?

Anakin Skywalker

➔ The Chosen One goes from strength to strength as his name becomes famous throughout the galaxy. His exploits are becoming legendary, but his fellow Jedi hope that having a Padawan will teach him to think before he acts.

Master Even Piell

➔ A fierce warrior and a skilled Force-user, Master Even Piell is a Lannik who was trained as a Jedi Knight from a young age. He has a reputation for never backing away from a fight, and is a member of the Jedi Council.

Master Plo Koon

➔ It was this Kel Dor Jedi Master who discovered Ahsoka Tano and recognised her strength in the Force. Master Plo Koon is a valuable member of the Jedi Council and a skilled starfighter pilot.

R2-D2

➔ There can be few astromech droids who have survived as many adventures as R2-D2, or who have as much personality. He is brave and loyal, with a wry sense of humour that is unusual in a droid.

C-3PO

➔ This protocol droid has an over-developed sense of doom, but he is devoted to his friends and will walk willingly into danger to help them. His loyalty to the Galactic Republic is matched only by his loyalty to the Skywalker clan.

PROFILES

Captain Tarkin

→ Wilhuff Tarkin serves as a captain under the command of Master Even Piell. He comes from a wealthy and powerful family, and has already had a successful political career. He is a great admirer and supporter of Supreme Chancellor Palpatine.

Osi Sobeck

→ This Phindian is the warden in charge of the notorious Citadel prison. He believes in using torture to get information from his enemies, and his cold yellow eyes show no mercy. He does not tolerate failure, and even his own troops are not safe from his cruelty.

Chewbacca

→ Wookiees are well-known for their great strength, and Chewbacca is no exception. He is also a skilled mechanic and one of the greatest warriors that his planet Kashyyyk has produced. He has a strong desire for adventure and exploration.

Commander Cody

→ A skilled clone trooper commander, Cody is proud to be serving under the command of Obi-Wan Kenobi. He is highly trained and greatly respected by his superiors.

Captain Rex

→ Serving under Anakin Skywalker, Rex is an independent and powerful trooper. He is not afraid to speak his mind and believes that experience outranks everything else. He considers his Jedi general a friend, and has guessed that Anakin is in love with Padmé Amidala.

Trandoshans

→ Throughout the galaxy, the Trandoshans are famous for their great strength and warlike culture. They are reptilian humanoids, that can re-grow lost limbs and regularly shed their skin.

Many Trandoshans become hunters, slavers and mercenaries. They believe in a goddess called the Scorekeeper, and they worship her by gaining jagannath points. These points are won through hunting and other aggressive acts. They have a variety of weapons to help them in their hunts.

Garnac

→ The leader of a Trandoshan slave ship.

Dar

→ Garnac's bloodthirsty son.

Lo Taren

→ A large and nasty Trandoshan hunter.

Tragon and Krix

→ Thugs under the command of Garnac.

Picture Quiz

1. Name the Species

Can you identify which species each of these photos shows?

A

B

C

D

2. Which Droid?

Can you name these different droid types?

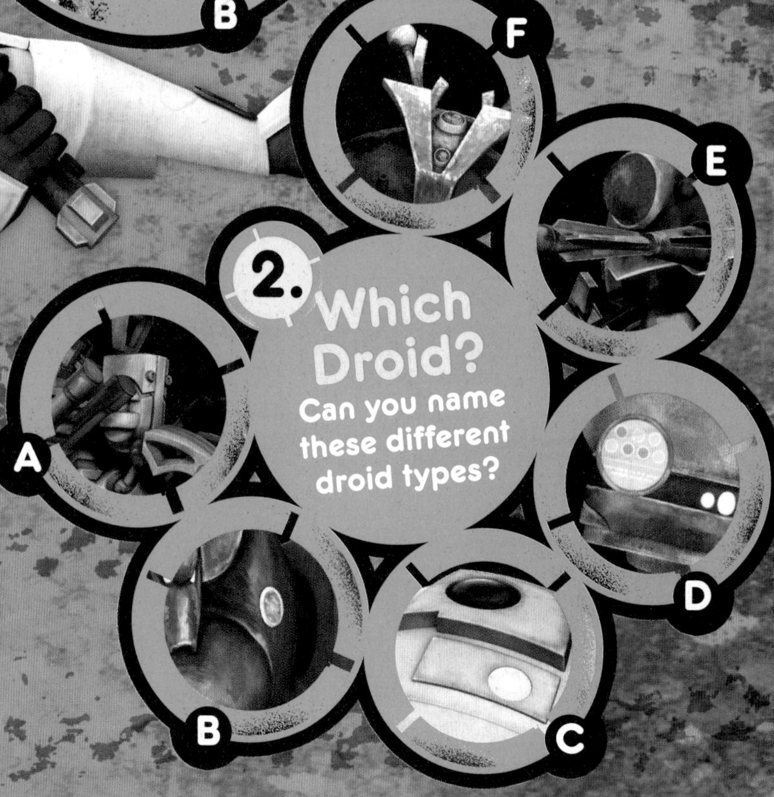

A

B

C

D

E

F

10

CLONE WARS

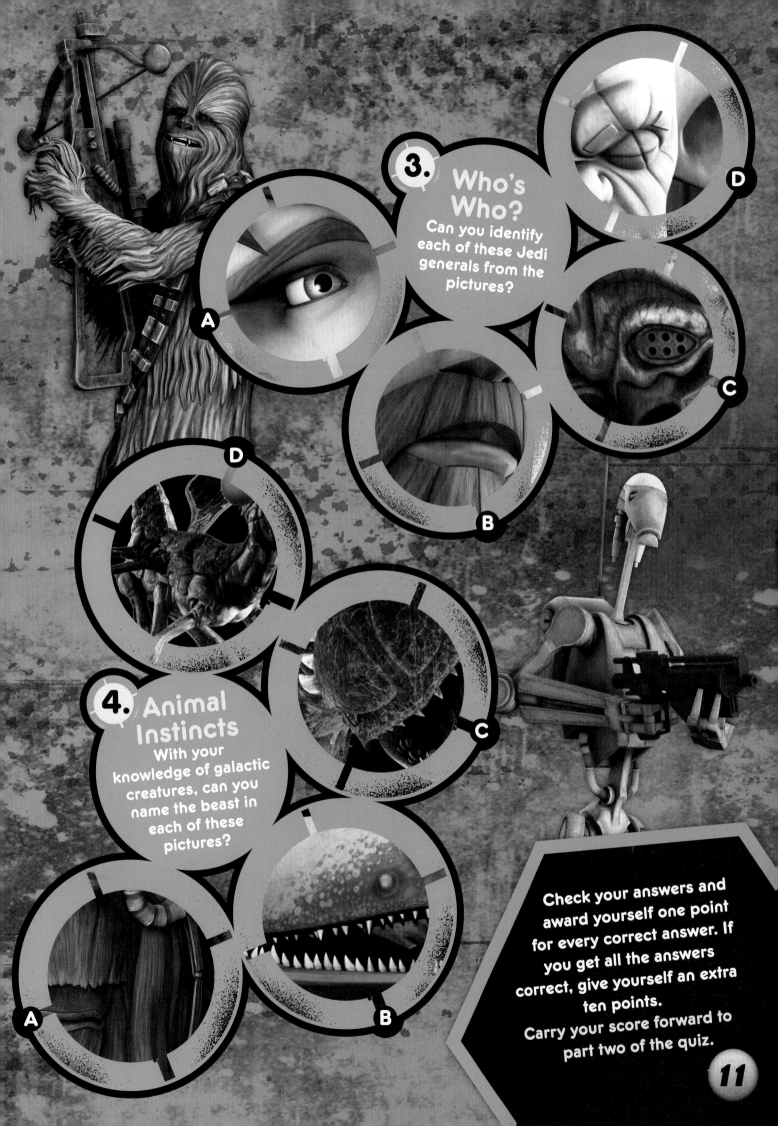

3.

Who's Who?
Can you identify each of these Jedi generals from the pictures?

A

B

C

D

4. **Animal Instincts**
With your knowledge of galactic creatures, can you name the beast in each of these pictures?

A

B

C

D

Check your answers and award yourself one point for every correct answer. If you get all the answers correct, give yourself an extra ten points.
Carry your score forward to part two of the quiz.

11

WORDSEARCH

The first names of twelve Jedi younglings and Masters are hidden in this grid. Can you locate them all?

```
K E K A B O T H I T N G M O M
O A Q O S X E R G I I H E B I
Y L L N N H O W K S N O M H T
B B C I E E M A R D I L Y A B
U U J S F B N P L I V I R E S
I K K R A A A H S O K A V F A
E P Y Y K R I R I P M S R M E
V I L Y R R O V E R S E P A U
E U O O B I W A N P H N R C M
N J F D B S N O R I M A B E B
L C W A Y S E F H E N U T A I
I Q Q M I M N A I I Q E H Q V
N C X P O E N U M X U O M Z Q
V Y T P M R G U T M I Y M M G
Z O X M E S L X Q P L M Y F O
```

AHSOKA	KALIFA	O-MER
JINX	BARRISS	LUMINARA
PLO	EVEN	ANAKIN
OBI-WAN	YODA	MACE

12

Jedi Hero

Use this grid to create your own picture of Obi-Wan Kenobi.

CLONE WARS

FIND THE JEDI

Four high-ranking Jedi are hiding in this busy scene. Can you locate and name them all?

STAR WARS THE CLONE WARS: THE CITADEL

Jedi Master Even Piell had been captured by Separatist forces. They wanted information from him, so they took him alive and locked him in the Citadel prison. He had the coordinates of a secret hyperspace lane called the Nexus route. It travelled into the heart of both the Republic and Separatist homeworlds, and whoever controlled it could tip the balance of the war in their favour.

A short time later, an elite Jedi force briefed their team on the rescue of Master Even Piell. No one had ever escaped from the Citadel, but as Master Anakin pointed out, there was a first time for everything.

"How do we know Master Piell is still alive?" asked Captain Rex.

"The Separatists won't dare kill Master Piell until they have what they need," said Obi-Wan.

After the briefing, the Jedi continued to make their plans.

"My greatest concern is infiltrating their outer security," Obi-Wan said. "The life form scanners will not be easy to fool."

At that moment Ahsoka came hurrying towards them.

"...just heard about the briefing," he said. "We're going to rescue Master Piell, right?"

Obi-Wan and Plo Koon looked at Anakin, and then left him alone with his Padawan.

"Ahsoka, I'm sorry I didn't tell you earlier, but you won't be coming along on this one," said Anakin, looking uncomfortable.

Ahsoka was very upset, but she could not change her Master's mind. Instead, she went to find her friend Master Plo Koon. She was hoping that she could persuade him to help her.

In the hangar, R2-D2 led three battle droids to the shuttle. They had been reprogrammed to follow his orders, as the Jedi were relying on them to fly them into the Citadel. The droids would not be detected, and the Jedi would be frozen in carbonite for the journey.

With the frozen Jedi safely on board, R2 and his battle droids flew the shuttle towards the massive planetoid, Lola Sayu. Destroyers and Dreadnoughts hovered nearby.

"Citadel command has contacted us," said the head battle droid, OOM-10, into his comlink. "This is cargo shuttle one, one, three, eight, requesting access to Citadel prison."

In the Citadel command centre, the prison warden Osi Sobeck was listening. "Make sure every part of that ship is scanned for life forms," he said. "The Jedi will be coming for their imprisoned brother."

"What is your cargo?" demanded a prison droid over the comlink.

"Supplies and frozen rations," said OOM-10.

"Do not deviate from your current course until we have confirmed your cargo," said the prison droid.

There was a long, tense silence as the prison computers began to scan the shuttle for life forms. After what seemed like forever, the life scan beeped negative and the shuttle was allowed to proceed.

The shuttle landed in one of the craggy canyons of Lola Sayu. In the background, on top of a mountain, was the imposing, heavily armed Citadel.

R2 de-thawed the Jedi team. As Obi-Wan and Anakin were unfrozen, they looked over and saw Ahsoka.

"I must have carbon sickness because I could swear that's Ahsoka," said Obi-Wan.

"Your eyes are fine," said Anakin grimly. "It's Ahsoka's hearing that needs help."

"I received orders to join the team," said Ahsoka. "I thought you knew."

"From who?" Anakin demanded.

"I discussed it with Master Plo," said Ahsoka.

Anakin was not happy, but there was nothing he could do about it now. The team set off for the Citadel and R2 stayed behind to guard the shuttle.

The team used their macrobinoculars to survey the Citadel. They saw that electro-mines were dotted around the surface of the mountain under the Citadel.

"There's nowhere to put a grappling hook at that height," said Anakin. "We hit one of those, the mission's over. They'll know we're here."

"I suppose that means we free-climb it," said Rex.

It was a long climb up the side of the mountain under the Citadel, battling against a high wind. At last they arrived at the entrance, but the door was locked and ray-shielded.

"There's an opening up there," said Ahsoka, pointing to a small ventilation duct near the entrance.

"Far too small for us to gain access," said Anakin.

"Too small for you maybe," said Ahsoka.

She climbed up to the duct and wiggled inside.

THE CITADEL

Inside the Citadel, Ahsoka emerged into a corridor. She quickly opened the door and the team started to enter. The wind was so strong that it was difficult to pull the last clones through. Suddenly, one of the clones slipped.

"Charger!" yelled Fives.

Charger tried to hold on, but he hit one of the mines and was electrocuted!

In the command centre, one of the battle droids noticed a problem.

"Sir, one of the cargo shuttles was cleared for landing but never arrived," he told Sobeck.

"A mine in sector nine-G was just detonated," said another battle droid.

"Activate all security protocols!" yelled Sobeck. "Lock everything down! Where are my special units?"

An alarm blared out and the Jedi team knew that they had been noticed. They raced deeper in to the Citadel, taking out the prison's surveillance units as they went. The walls began to vibrate and a surge of electricity crackled down the hallway towards them. Everyone ran for cover, but one trooper couldn't make it in time. They had lost another team member.

In an interrogation chamber, squads of commando droids were standing guard as a torture droid prodded Even Piell with an electric staff.

"You're weakening," said the droid. "You decide when the pain will stop. Just give me the information."

Piell looked up with his one good eye.

"No droid will ever break me," he said.

The door blasted open and the Jedi team raced into the room, lightsabers ablaze. They cut down the droids and released Piell. He told them that he had half the coordinates for the Nexus Route.

"My captain's got the other half," he explained. "I erased the computers when we were boarded and had both of us memorise part of the intel. That way, if somehow I cracked, the information would be useless to them without the other half."

"Where's your captain?" asked Obi-Wan.

"Being held with the other officers, I assume," said Even.

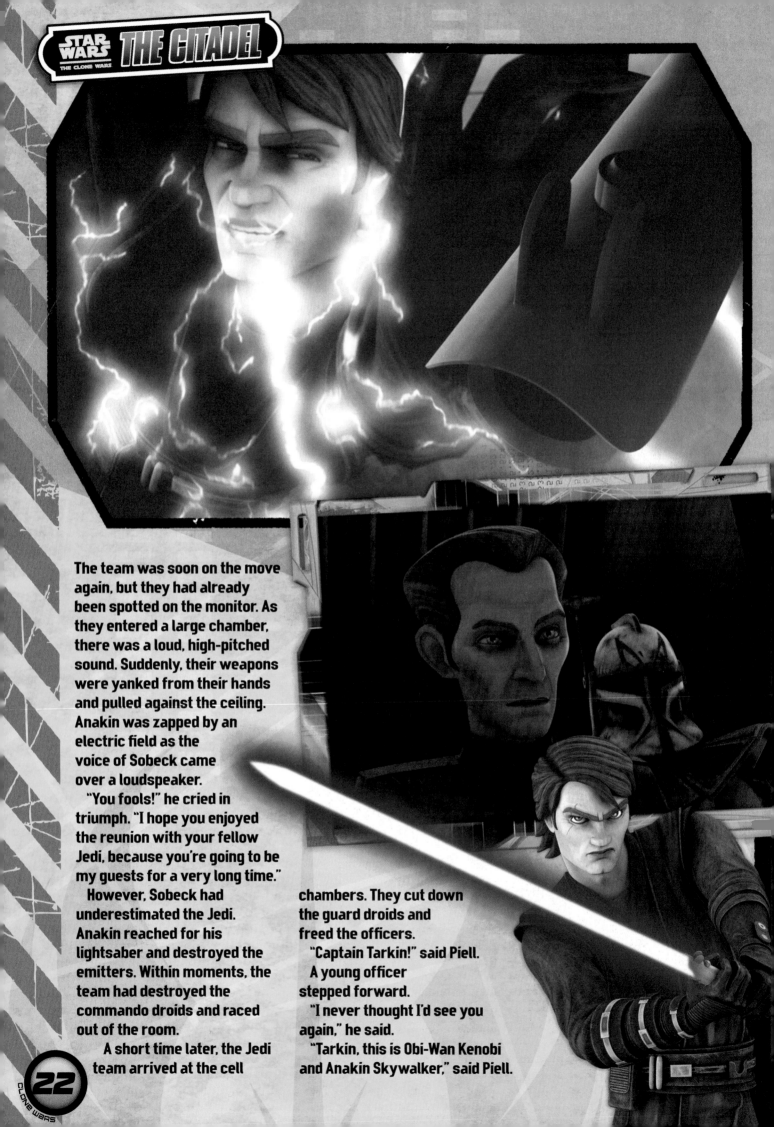

The team was soon on the move again, but they had already been spotted on the monitor. As they entered a large chamber, there was a loud, high-pitched sound. Suddenly, their weapons were yanked from their hands and pulled against the ceiling. Anakin was zapped by an electric field as the voice of Sobeck came over a loudspeaker.

"You fools!" he cried in triumph. "I hope you enjoyed the reunion with your fellow Jedi, because you're going to be my guests for a very long time."

However, Sobeck had underestimated the Jedi. Anakin reached for his lightsaber and destroyed the emitters. Within moments, the team had destroyed the commando droids and raced out of the room.

A short time later, the Jedi team arrived at the cell chambers. They cut down the guard droids and freed the officers.

"Captain Tarkin!" said Piell.

A young officer stepped forward.

"I never thought I'd see you again," he said.

"Tarkin, this is Obi-Wan Kenobi and Anakin Skywalker," said Piell.

Tarkin stared at them coldly.

"Now that you've found us, how do you expect to get us out?" he asked. "If they've locked this fortress down there's at least ten squads on their way. It's going to be impossible to escape."

"What if we split up?" Obi-Wan suggested. "My team will create a diversion, while Anakin leads the others away. That way, if one of us is captured, the enemy will only have part of the information and not all of it."

"General Kenobi, I think it's better if we stick together," said Tarkin. "A stronger force would have a better chance of protecting the information."

"Obi-Wan has a point," said Piell. "I'll go with him, you go with Skywalker."

Obi-Wan and Piell led their team in one direction, planting thermal detonators as they went. They

set off a series of explosions that ripped through the lower levels of the Citadel.

Anakin led his team in the opposite direction. He checked his holographic map, stopped and cut a large hole in the wall with his lightsaber. Everyone

climbed through and they found themselves in a tunnel. It was one of the original fortress tunnels.

He looked at Tarkin. It was clear that the captain didn't trust him. But for now, things were going as planned.

STORY CONTINUED PAGE 28

23

ANIMAL ATTACK

There are many different types of hunters in the galaxy. Solve these clues to find the names of predators from the planet Earth.

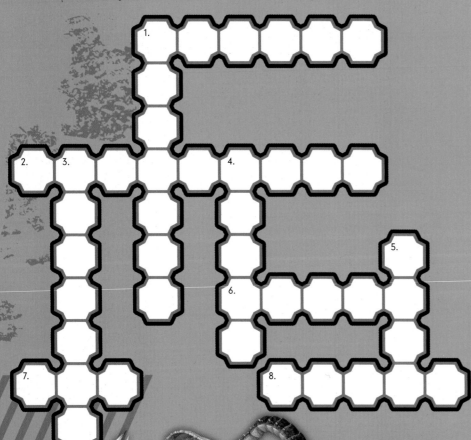

ACROSS

1. A snake that kills its prey by squeezing them to death
2. An eight-legged creature that dissolves its prey with digestive juices
6. A large bird of prey
7. A house pet that preys on mice and birds
8. An ocean-dwelling predator with serrated teeth
9. A bird that hunts at night
11. A four-legged animal that hunts in a pack

DOWN

1. A fish with slicing teeth and powerful jaws
3. This reptile lurks in the water and kills its prey with bone-crushing bites
4. A stripy feline that is the national animal of India
5. A grizzly animal with strong limbs and huge clawed paws
10. The king of the jungle
12. A mammal with reddish fur and a long bushy tail

ODD ONE OUT

These pictures of Captain Rex look the same, but one of them is slightly different. Can you find the odd one out?

HOW TO DRAW
Chewbacca

Follow these steps and learn how to draw this hairy co-pilot.

1

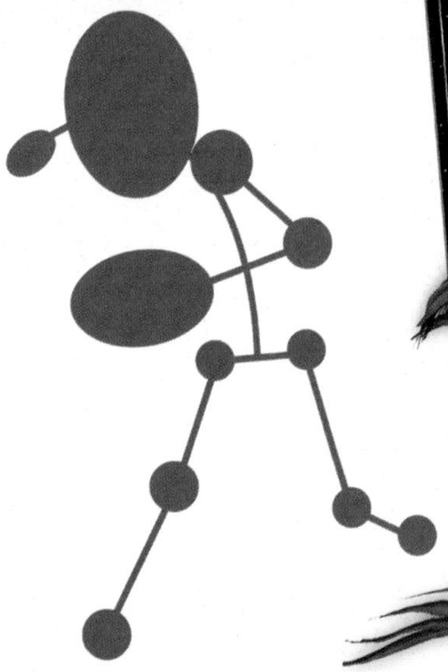

Use lines and circles to create Chewbacca's shape and pose.

2

Fill out the head and body shape with light pencil lines.

3

Gradually add the detail of Chewbacca's fur and expression.

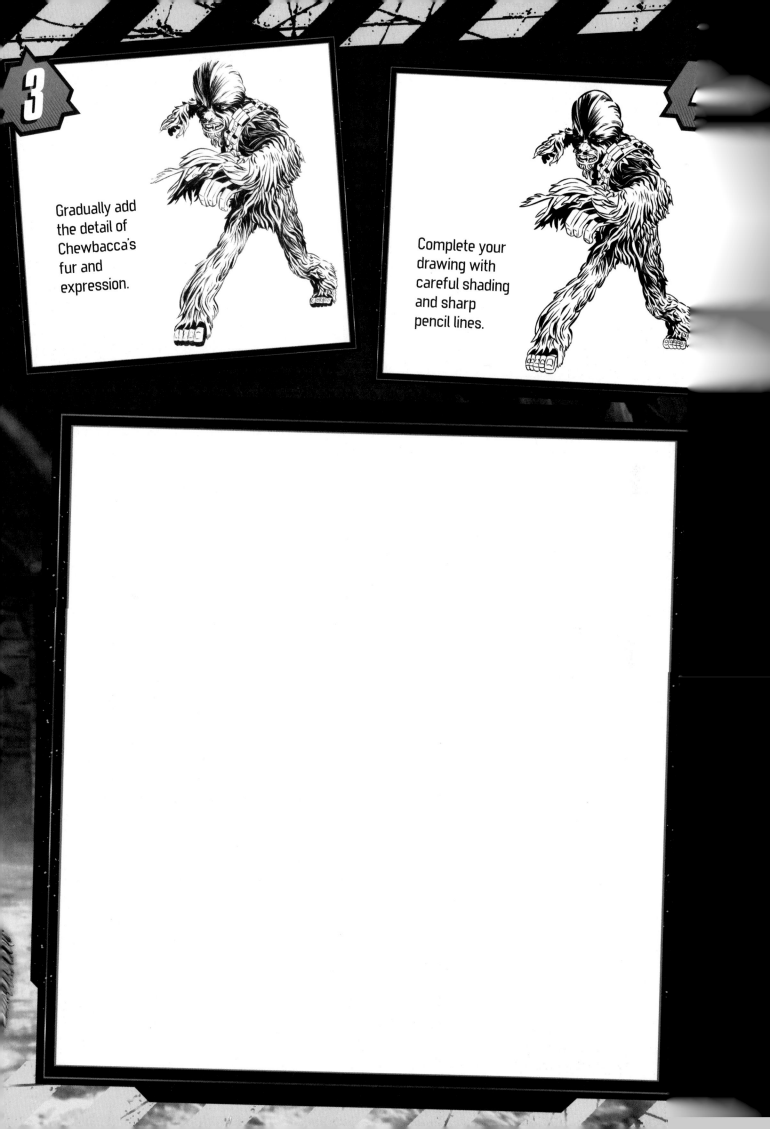

Complete your drawing with careful shading and sharp pencil lines.

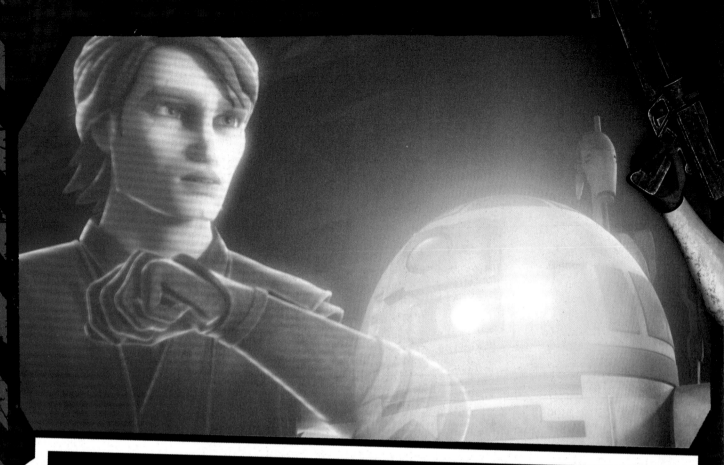

STAR WARS

THE CLONE WARS

COUNTER ATTACK

nside the fortress tunnel, Anakin's team was heading for the pipeline exit. Anakin spoke to R2 over the comlink and asked him to bring the ship to the rendezvous point.

"I am beginning to admire the design of this fortress," said Tarkin as they trekked down the dimly lit tunnel.

"How can you admire such a horrible place?" asked Ahsoka.

"You reveal your short-sightedness," Tarkin replied. "This ordeal only demonstrates how effective facilities like the Citadel are. Pity it ended up in Separatist hands and not ours."

"He has a point," said Anakin. "All right, Snips, I need you to lead the group. Keep following the tunnel. I'll catch up."

"Where are you going?" asked Ahsoka in surprise.

"Obi-Wan's not here, so someone has to protect our flank," her Master replied.

Ahsoka beamed with pride.

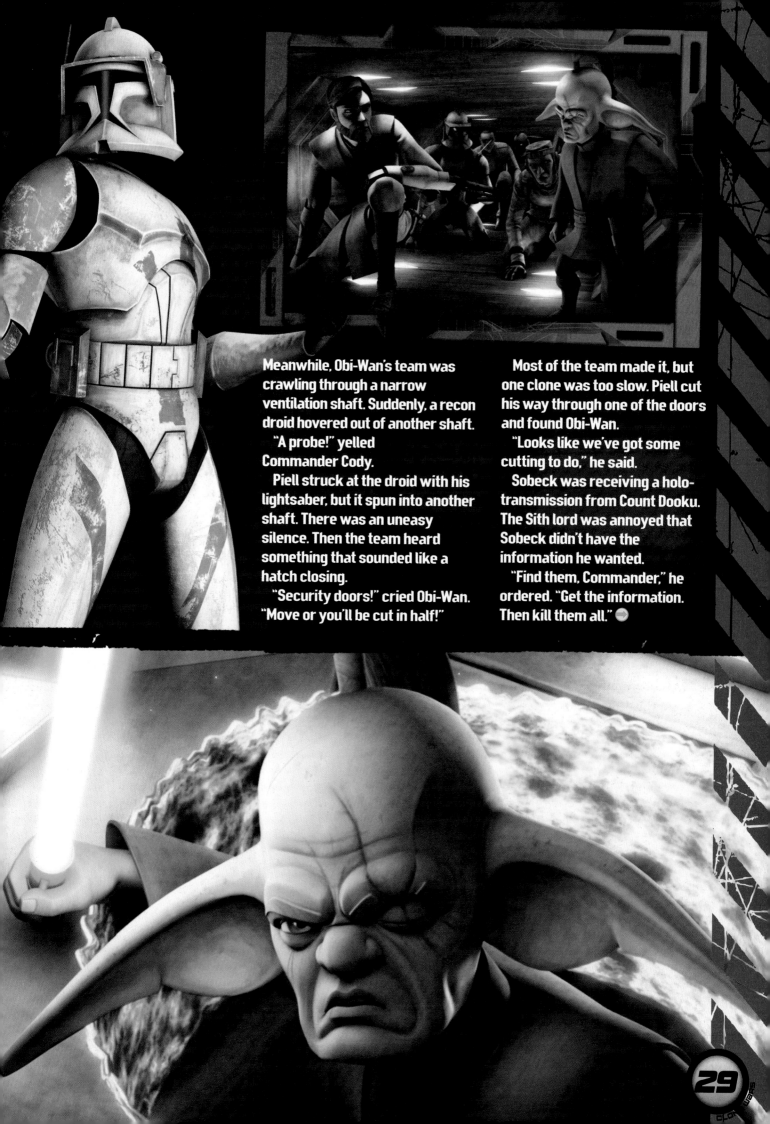

Meanwhile, Obi-Wan's team was crawling through a narrow ventilation shaft. Suddenly, a recon droid hovered out of another shaft.

"A probe!" yelled Commander Cody.

Piell struck at the droid with his lightsaber, but it spun into another shaft. There was an uneasy silence. Then the team heard something that sounded like a hatch closing.

"Security doors!" cried Obi-Wan. "Move or you'll be cut in half!"

Most of the team made it, but one clone was too slow. Piell cut his way through one of the doors and found Obi-Wan.

"Looks like we've got some cutting to do," he said.

Sobeck was receiving a holo-transmission from Count Dooku. The Sith lord was annoyed that Sobeck didn't have the information he wanted.

"Find them, Commander," he ordered. "Get the information. Then kill them all."

As Ahsoka led the team deeper into a narrow passage, Tarkin leaned closer to Rex.

"I am concerned that the Jedi have elected this child to lead the group," he hissed.

"I've served with her many times and I trust her, Captain," replied Rex.

Before Tarkin could say anything else, Ahsoka stopped. They had come to a dead end. While she was trying to decide what to do, her team came under attack by commando droids.

Anakin rejoined the team.

"What happened?" he demanded. "Why didn't you blow the wall?"

"I thought it was a dead end," said Ahsoka, confused.

If Master Plo really assigned you to this mission, he would have briefed you on the plan,"

Anakin snapped.

Ahsoka placed thermal detonators around the wall, using two on the commando droids. She activated the detonators, clearing the exit and the droids. Then the team entered the fuel line that would lead them towards their meeting point with R2.

Outside the Citadel, R2's battle droids landed the shuttle on the rooftop and a prison droid marched up to them. He suspected that R2 was a traitor, but he didn't know that the battle droids had been reprogrammed! He ordered them to take R2 to the interrogation room.

Obi-Wan and his team left the ventilation shaft, thinking that they would find R2 waiting for them. Instead, they were surrounded by droids, who took them to the command centre.

"I want your half of the information," growled Sobeck. "Give it to me now, or I'll start executing your men."

"This is war, Sobeck," said Piell. "We're all prepared to die to protect that intel."

Sobeck blasted a clone trooper dead. He was about to kill another when one of his droids interrupted.

"Sir, we have located the other group and our droids are closing in on them."

"Your Jedi resolve only delays the inevitable," sneered Sobeck. "Take them to Interrogation. Torture them slowly." ➡

Elsewhere in the Citadel, R2 used a computer port to find out where Obi-Wan's team was being taken. He sent his battle droids to rescue them, and tricked the real prison battle droids into handing the Jedi team over. Soon they were all heading back to the shuttle, confident that Anakin would switch to plan B.

Anakin was leading his team along the dark tunnel and chatting to Tarkin. They shared some doubts about Jedi methods, but before they could talk further, Ahsoka found an exit hatch. She poked her head up out of it.

"Any sign of Obi-Wan and the shuttle?" asked Anakin.

"No, I don't see him or Artoo anywhere," she replied.

Suddenly, a droid blaster appeared at her head. She sliced the droids apart, but there were more on their way.

"We've got to go!" she yelled.

"There could be a whole battalion of droids out there!" exclaimed Tarkin.

"Better than hiding in a fuel line," said Anakin.

Everyone climbed out, and came immediately under fire. They scattered behind rocks as the droids advanced on them. But when the droids marched over the fuel pipe, Anakin threw a detonator into the open hatch. BOOM! A massive blast wiped out the droids.

"Let's go!" said Anakin. "Time for plan B."

In the command centre, Sobeck was glaring at a holographic map of the area. Things were going badly wrong. Obi-Wan's team had escaped, his droids had failed to capture Anakin's team and now Count Dooku was demanding that he make contact.

"Inform Count Dooku that I am unreachable," he ordered. "Send all units to the airfield – it's their only possible way of escape."

R2's droids were approaching the landing field with Obi-Wan's team. Prison droids were guarding the shuttle. As they challenged the team, Obi-Wan's lightsaber started to slash at them. Anakin's team arrived from the other side and a battalion of commando droids poured into the fray. A battle was underway.

The shuttle was surrounded, and Tarkin wanted to launch a full forward assault. But they also had to take out the gun turrets, otherwise they could be used to destroy the shuttle.

"Whatever we're going to do, we'd better do it fast," said Anakin.

A group of droids was bearing down on them on STAPs.

Anakin seized a STAP and Piell leaped up beside him. One commando droid raced towards the gun turrets and Echo chased him. The commando droid saw him and fired.

"Echo, look out!" yelled Fives.

It was too late. The shuttle exploded and debris hit the turret as Echo's charred helmet fell to the ground.

"We have to go now!" exclaimed Obi-Wan.

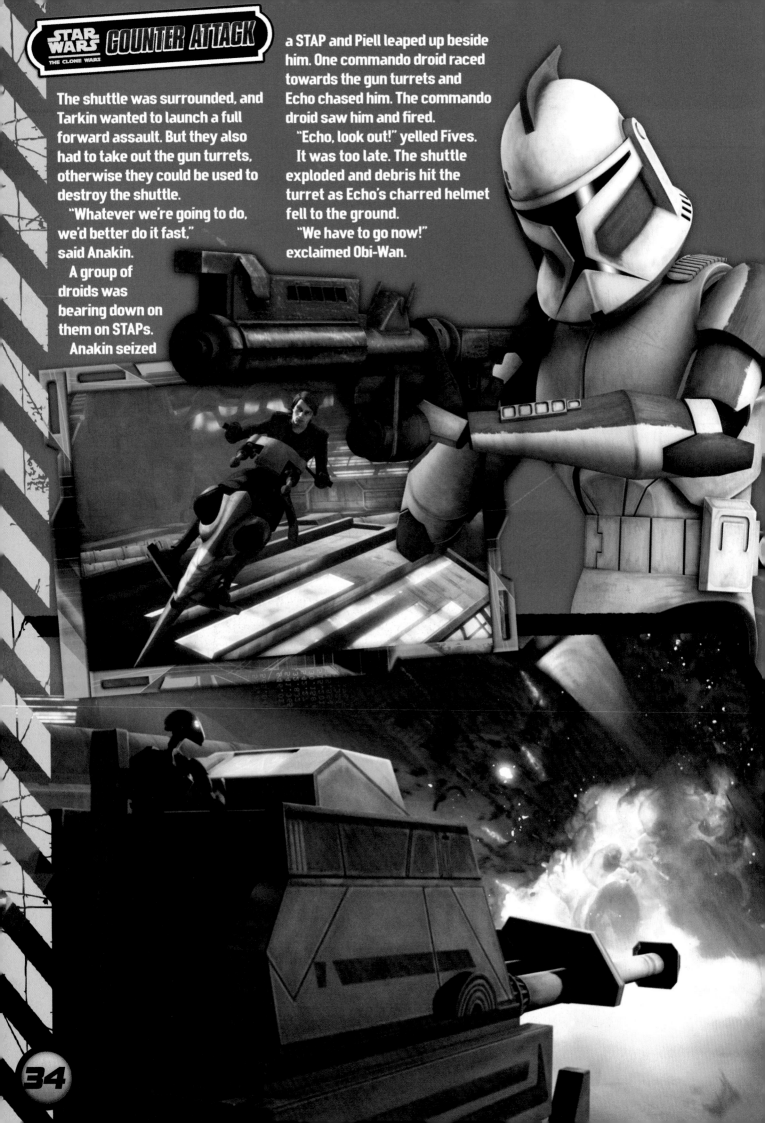

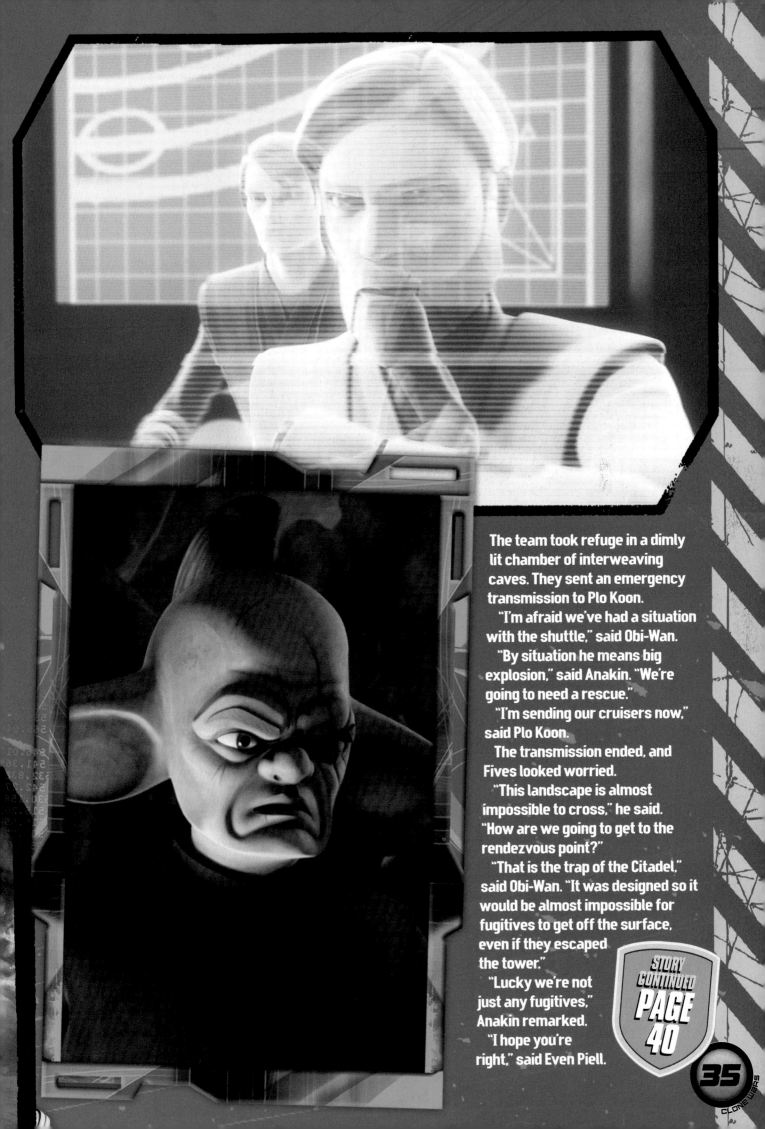

The team took refuge in a dimly lit chamber of interweaving caves. They sent an emergency transmission to Plo Koon.

"I'm afraid we've had a situation with the shuttle," said Obi-Wan.

"By situation he means big explosion," said Anakin. "We're going to need a rescue."

"I'm sending our cruisers now," said Plo Koon.

The transmission ended, and Fives looked worried.

"This landscape is almost impossible to cross," he said. "How are we going to get to the rendezvous point?"

"That is the trap of the Citadel," said Obi-Wan. "It was designed so it would be almost impossible for fugitives to get off the surface, even if they escaped the tower."

"Lucky we're not just any fugitives," Anakin remarked.

"I hope you're right," said Even Piell.

STORY CONTINUED PAGE 40

35

Shadowplay

Your challenge is to identify these famous Jedi
from their shadows alone. Which Jedi is which?

Dot to Dot

Which wise leader is hidden in this picture?
Join the dots to find out.

ESCAPE FROM THE CITADEL

Can you escape from the vile Citadel prison?

YOU WILL NEED:
Dice • Counters

HOW TO PLAY:
Ask each player to choose a counter and decide who will go first.

Throw the dice and move the counter along the board.

If you land on a ladder, climb up the board. If you land on a chute, slide down the board.

The winner is the first player to reach the escape ship.

FINISH
100

98

99

81   82   83   8

80   79   78

6

61   62   63   6

60   59   58

You discover your friends. Go forward three spaces.

42   43   4

41

40   38

39

21   22   23   24

20

19   18

START
1   2   3   4

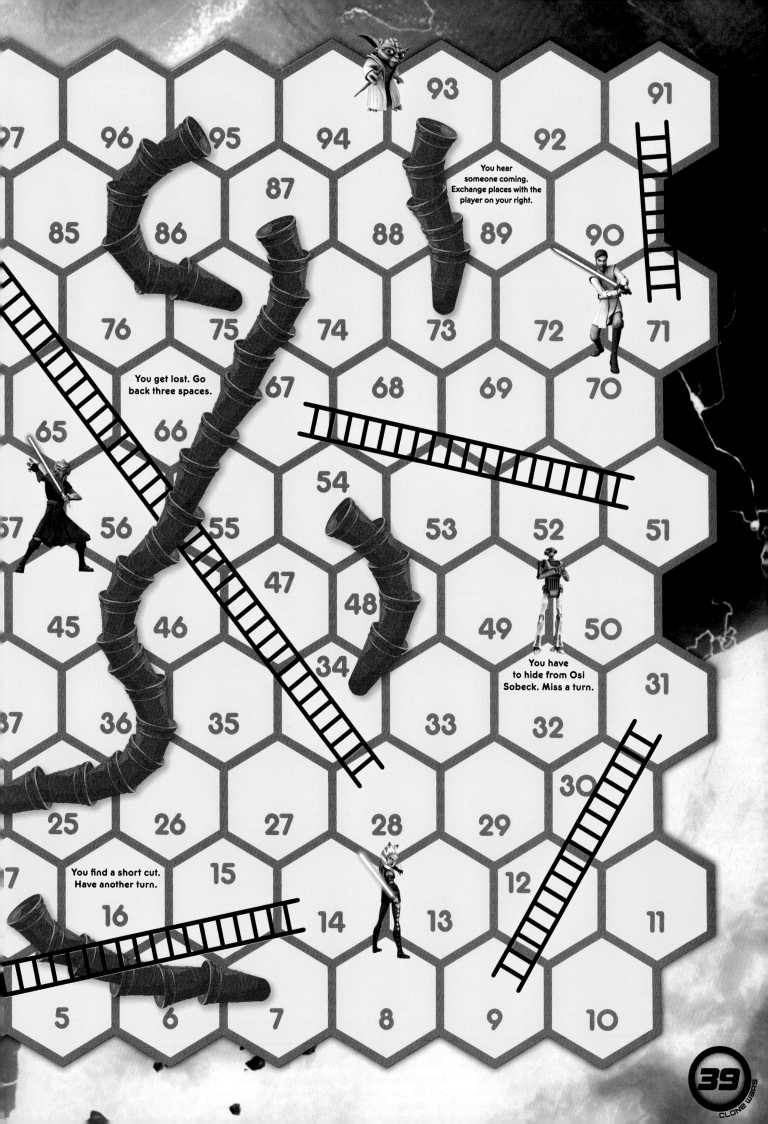

STAR WARS
THE CLONE WARS
CITADEL RESCUE

T he Jedi rescue team was waiting to be rescued by the Jedi Council, and Plo Koon was already on his way with gunships. The rendezvous point was a small island – but they would have to fight their way there.

Osi Sobeck was in the command centre. A hologram of Dooku appeared as a column of droids marched in the background.

"Have the prisoners been captured?" Dooku demanded.

"Not yet, my lord," Sobeck replied. "But we've located their position and my droids are moving in now.

"I need not remind you that the prisoners are carrying secret hyperspace coordinates into the core systems of the Republic and our Separatist homeworlds," said Dooku grimly. "This information will allow us to launch a surprise attack on Coruscant."

"I will see to it that they are soon back in our possession," Sobeck assured him.

"Right now your honesty is the only thing keeping you alive," said Dooku.

The Jedi team was moving along the narrow ledge as crab droids climbed down the canyon walls, boxing them in. Below them was a sheer drop of thousands of feet.

"Lock in your cables," said Anakin. "Artoo, we need your droids to hold off the enemy as long as possible."

While the battle droids held off the enemy for as long as they could, the team walked face-first down the side of the cliff, strapped to cables. R2 rocketed down beside the Jedi. They had to keep moving.

Meanwhile, four Jedi cruisers were blasting through hyperspace. Jedi Masters Plo Koon, Adi Gallia, Saesee Tiin and Kit Fisto were on their way to rescue their friends. Saesee Tiin would lead the fighter attack while Plo Koon led the gunships down to the surface. ➡

As the team travelled over the jagged, pock-marked wasteland, Tarkin was still voicing his doubts.

"What if your Jedi friends are not there when we arrive?" he asked.

"Keep moving and you won't have to worry about that, Tarkin," said Piell.

Ahsoka rolled her eyes. She didn't like Tarkin.

"Why did Master Piell have to share half of the intel with that guy?" she asked. "It's like he's not even grateful we rescued him."

"Captain Tarkin feels the Jedi should be relieved from the burden of leading the war effort," said Anakin. "The Jedi code often prevents us from going far enough to achieve victory."

"A rather simple point of view," said Obi-Wan.

"Either way, he is a good captain," said Anakin.

They were interrupted by the sound of howling in the distance. Sobeck had sent out anoobas to hunt the team down.

"We're going to have company," said Piell.

High above the planetoid, a blockade of Separatist ships was patrolling Lola Sayu. Osi Sobeck had ordered them to ensure that any rescue attempts by the Jedi would fail.

The team made its way over a field of razor-sharp craters and bubbling pools of sulphur. They had to keep moving – if they missed the rendezvous time, they might never be rescued. But the anoobas were tracking them, and their howls were getting louder.

"If they've caught our scent, they'll lead the droids right to us," said Even Piell.

"We're going to have to deal with them," said Anakin.

Ahsoka spotted a cave.

"What about using this cave to surprise them?" she suggested.

"If we can get them to pass by, we can attack them from behind," said Even Piell. "But we need a distraction."

Piell, Ahsoka, Tarkin and the clones went into the cave while Obi-Wan and Anakin charged ahead with R2 to distract the anoobas. The Jedi fought the beasts as STAPs appear and blasted at them. ➲

Crab droids attacked the rest of the team, and Piell ordered the clones to leave.

"Keep going!" he said. "Ahsoka and I will take care of the droids."

They went, and Piell sliced through the droids. But then a yellow-eyed anooba hurled itself at him, throwing him into the air.

"Master Piell!" screamed Ahsoka.

She destroyed the last droid and then Force-pushed the anooba into the lava. But Piell was badly hurt. He clasped her arm.

"The information . . ." he gasped. "I need you to deliver it back to the Council."

"I should find Anakin or Obi-Wan," cried Ahsoka.

Tarkin and the clones joined Obi-Wan and Anakin, and together they battled furiously until they were surrounded by the bodies of dead anoobas and the wreckage of STAPs. They had won, but Obi-Wan's face fell when he saw the lone figure of Ahsoka appear on the hill, carrying the body of Master Even Piell.

"He died honourably," said Ahsoka.

"What about the information?" Anakin asked.

"I have it," said Ahsoka. "He told me . . . just before he died."

The team used the Force to place Piell's body into the river of lava, and then moved on. They knew that he had wanted them to complete their mission.

Above Lola Sayu, the four Jedi cruisers emerged from hyperspace and opened fire on the Separatist ships. A massive space battle began, and the Jedi forces were struggling to get through the blockade.

"We're out of time, Master Tiin," said Plo Koon. "We must break through now."

"Wing commanders form up," said Saesee Tiin. "We're going in." ➡

The rendezvous point was in the middle of a fiery lake of lava. The team fired cables across the lava to the island, and one by one they started to shimmy across. But Sobeck and his droids were close behind them.

Most of the team reached the island, but Ahsoka was still on the wire when Sobeck swooped down to blast her. Suddenly, R2 sprayed him with a smoke screen from a side panel! Sobeck swerved and Fives fired, forcing the prison warden to crash land on the island. He found Tarkin and lifted him up to throw him into the lava.

"If I can't have the information it will die with you!" he yelled.

But before he could complete his threat, he was killed by Ahsoka's lightsaber.

"My thanks, Padawan Tano," said Tarkin.

At that moment the Jedi gunship dropped out of the sky.

"I believe you've worn out your welcome," said Plo Koon.

The team dived into the gunship and it lifted off at once. Under heavy fire, it held its course and swooped into a cruiser. Then all four Jedi cruisers launched into hyperspace. The rescue had succeeded!

When the Jedi arrived back on Coruscant, Yoda and Mace Windu were waiting for them. They were saddened to hear of Piell's loss, but thanks to him they had the Nexus Route coordinates.

"Captain Tarkin and Ahsoka have each memorised half," Obi-Wan explained.

"Debrief them both, we must," said Yoda.

"With all due respect, Master Jedi, I was instructed by Chancellor Palpatine to bring the intel directly to him for debriefing," said Tarkin.

"I promised Master Piell that I would deliver it only to the Council," said Ahsoka. "And that's what I will do."

Obi-Wan shared her mistrust of Tarkin, but Anakin saw him as a new ally.

"I think we need people like him," he said. "This is a war. If we aren't willing to do what it takes to win, we risk losing everything we try to protect."

His Master gazed thoughtfully at him.

"War tends to distort our point of view," said Obi-Wan. "If we sacrifice our code, even for victory, we may lose that which is most important – our honour."

Sudoku Challenge

9								
	7	5	4					
3			6	2	9			5
	5		9		7			
								3
6	3				2			
						5		4
	4		3	1		7		
7						2		

Can you complete this number puzzle? Fill in all the empty squares so that every row, every column and every 3x3 square contain the numbers 1 to 9.

DARK SIDE PUZZLE

Turn sleep into dream by solving the clues and changing one letter at a time.

S	L	E	E	P
1.				
2.				
3.				
4.				
5.				

D	R	E	A	M

1 One of the sounds that R2-D2 makes

2 What a living creature does if they are wounded

3 A word that means having offspring

4 Something you need to make a sandwich

5 A feeling of doom and fear

Picture Quiz

Part 2

1. Symbol Sorter
What do these symbols stand for?

A

B

C

D

2. Senate Members
Can you identify the Senators in these pictures?

A

B

C

D

50

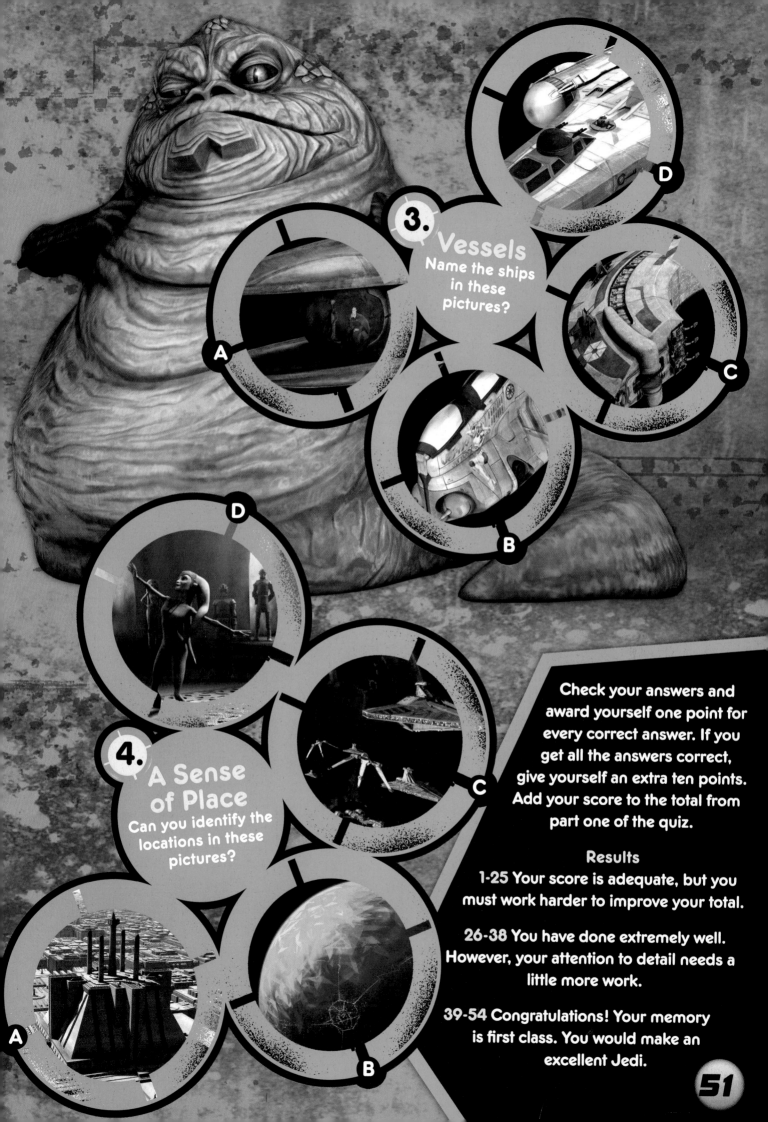

3.

Vessels
Name the ships in these pictures?

A

B

C

D

4.

A Sense of Place
Can you identify the locations in these pictures?

A

B

C

D

Check your answers and award yourself one point for every correct answer. If you get all the answers correct, give yourself an extra ten points. Add your score to the total from part one of the quiz.

Results
1-25 Your score is adequate, but you must work harder to improve your total.

26-38 You have done extremely well. However, your attention to detail needs a little more work.

39-54 Congratulations! Your memory is first class. You would make an excellent Jedi.

STAR WARS
THE CLONE WARS
PADAWAN LOST

In the Outer Rim, the planet Felucia was caught between Republic and Separatist forces. Anakin Skywalker and Ahsoka Tano were leading clone tank divisions into Separatist-controlled territory, and General Grievous had already sent reinforcements to one of his droid outposts. Plo Koon, Anakin and Ahsoka watched them arrive through macrobinoculars.

"We shall break into three groups to divide their defences," said Plo Koon. "I'll take the left flank, Skywalker attack the front gate, Ahsoka you scale the back wall. We'll meet in the middle."

Soon the Jedi were on the move, each followed by their troops. Ahsoka was making her way through a forest with Comet and her other clone troopers.

As soon as all the Jedi troops were in position, they opened fire on the droid outpost. Anakin, Plo Koon and their troops joined the battle. Then it was Ahsoka's turn. Her troopers shot grappling cables up the wall while she stayed at the base and protected their flank.

As soon as her troopers were clear, Ahsoka switched off her lightsaber and prepared to follow them up. She turned – and was knocked out by an energy net. Lo-Taren, a large and nasty Trandoshan, stood over her body.

"I can't believe my luck," he said. "A Jedi youngling."

At the droid outpost, Anakin, Plo Koon and the clones finished off the remaining droids and seized control. It was only then that they realised Ahsoka was missing.

"Everybody fan out," Anakin ordered. "I want a perimeter sweep, now."

Ahsoka awoke in the dark, damp hold of a Trandoshan slave ship. She found herself in a rusted metal cage beside another prisoner – a Snivvian.

"What is this place?" she asked. "Who are these pirates?"

"These are Trandoshans," replied the Snivvian. "They're going to release us and hunt us down for sport." ➡

53

Two Trandoshan thugs called Lagon and Krix were sitting at the ship's controls. Behind them was Garnac, their leader, and his son Dar. Lo-Taren joined them.

"We have found new prey for the hunt," he said. "The youngling will provide great sport."

"Perhaps your first Jedi kill," Garnac suggested to his son.

"She'll die by my claw!" hissed Dar eagerly.

A short time later, the slave ship arrived at Wasskah, the Trandoshan moon. It hovered above an island and dropped the prisoners to the beach below, opening fire on them as they scrambled for cover.

Ahsoka escaped into the jungle, but she wasn't alone for long. She met three Jedi younglings who took her to a hidden cave. They had been attacked on a training mission and brought to the island. The Trandoshans targeted younglings because Jedi were too powerful for them.

"I'm Kalifa," said the human girl, introducing the Cerean as O-Mer and the Twi'lek as Jinx. "Who are you?"

"Ahsoka Tano," the Togrutan replied. "I was captured during the battle of Felucia. I'm a Padawan learner. What's the situation here?"

"You'd better sit down," said Kalifa. "We were taken by those foul lizards for their amusement. To be hunted, killed, and mounted on their wall as trophies."

At dawn the next day, Ahsoka was shaken out of her sleep by Kalifa.

"Ahsoka, it's time to go," she said. "The sun's almost up, which means we clear out."

"Where do you go?" asked Ahsoka.

"We keep moving and keep those disgusting hunters from picking up our scent," Kalifa replied.

It didn't seem like much of a plan to Ahsoka, but she followed the other Padawans out of the cave and back into the jungle.

The Trandoshans were awake too. Dar, Garnac and Lo-Taren had been joined by several more hunters.

"The sun has risen," said Garnac. "Let the hunt begin!"

They howled and snarled as they entered hover pods and flew down to the island.

The Padawans were moving through the upper layer of the jungle when they saw two more prisoners walking through the forest. Ahsoka wanted to help them, but suddenly a shot rang out – the Trandoshans were on the hunt. Kalifa ordered Ahsoka and the others to hide as the two prisoners were killed.

"We'll never get out of here if we just keep hiding," Ahsoka said. "We have to act."

"There were other Padawans here that once thought as you do," said Jinx.

"Where are they?" Ahsoka demanded.

"They're dead," said Kalifa.

But Ahsoka knew that Anakin would never forgive her for running and hiding in a situation like this. She set off towards the Trandoshans alone, and before long she was attacked by Lo-Taren. He overpowered her and threw her to the ground. But as he stood over her, he started to choke. He dropped his gun and lifted off the ground. Kalifa was standing behind him, anger in her eyes. This was Jedi power.

"Don't kill him out of hatred," said Ahsoka. "It's not the Jedi way."

Kalifa lowered Lo-Taren to the ground and he cried out for help. Ahsoka picked up his blaster and ran back to the cave with the others.

Ahsoka was frustrated to find that the blaster didn't work. The Trandoshans deactivated blasters if they were taken. But her actions had awoken something in the other Padawans.

"Ahsoka, your energy, your strength, it's what we've been lacking," said Kalifa. "We were beginning to lose hope and forgot who we are."

Ahsoka suggested that they should try to find out where the Trandoshans lived. They would start their search in the morning. ➲

The next day, the Padawans searched the beach area and most of the briar on their side of the bay. But the Trandoshan base was nowhere to be seen.

"If it was easy to find, you guys would have found it before I got here," Ahsoka remarked. "Maybe we should try more inland?"

O-Mer was sitting back, his head to the sky. Suddenly his expression changed from one of rest to surprise and awe.

"Guys, I think we're looking in the wrong place," he said. "That's their fortress!"

The Jedi looked up and saw the looming hunting lodge platform. Hover pods zoomed towards them as laser fire rained down.

"Split up!" yelled Kalifa.

She vaulted through the upper canopy and ran across the thorn vine trails, chased by Dar and Garnac in a pod. Laser fire hit the branch beneath her, and she fell to the jungle floor far below. Dar leaped from the pod, determined to kill her with his own hands.

"You have the honour of being my first Jedi kill," hissed Dar, gazing down at the Padawan. "First of many, I hope!"

He aimed his blaster at Kalifa, but at that moment Ahsoka dropped down upon him. They struggled through the canopy, and then as Dar hurled himself at her, she vaulted aside. The young Trandoshan plunged to his death.

Kalifa had a broken arm. Ahsoka helped her up, but they had forgotten that Garnac was still inside the pod. A fatal shot rang out and Kalifa went pale. She had been hit.

"Those Jedi whelps killed my son!" they heard Garnac wail. "There's no escape! I'll hunt you down!"

"Leave me," gasped Kalifa.

"I won't," said Ahsoka.

But Kalifa knew that she was dying.

"Ahsoka," she said, "please take care …"

"I'll take care of the others," Ahsoka promised.

Kalifa took her last breath, and then died in the high canopy. Ahsoka ran off into the jungle with Garnac's roars ringing in her ears.

"You killed my son!" he cried. "I'll kill you! You can't hide from me!"

STORY CONTINUED PAGE 64

PRISON PIECES

Which jigsaw puzzle pieces complete the puzzle picture of the Citadel prison? Draw lines to place them in the correct spaces.

E

F

G

H

COLOUR BY

Use the code at the bottom of the page to complete this picture of Ahsoka's adventures with her Jedi friends.

NUMBERS

STAR WARS
THE CLONE WARS
WOOKIE HUNT

Ahsoka made her way back to the hidden cave, relieved but exhausted. O-Mer and Jinx were sitting by the fire.

"You made it!" exclaimed Jinx in relief. "Where's Kalifa?"

Sadly, Ahsoka told them about Kalifa's death. They were shocked.

"We're all going to die here," said O-Mer. "It's only a matter of time."

"If it's only a matter of time till we die, I say we go down with a fight," Ahsoka replied. "You've said that every few days they release new prisoners on the beach. I say we attack that drop ship, head on. They'll never expect it."

It was definitely worth a shot.

early morning mist, Ahsoka, and Jinx hid at the edge of the n. They could hear an incoming ship. As it hovered at the edge e water, the Padawans raced ss the beach and leaped onto it. Trandoshans inside – Goron and ch – gave cries of surprise. ron opened the hatch and aimed hsoka, but he was hit from ind by O-Mer. Jinx joined the fight

and Clutch fell back against the controls, sending the ship into a spin.

The Trandoshans and Padawans wrestled as the ship tumbled out of control. At last Clutch and Goron were thrown from the ship, but the fight had damaged it beyond repair. The Padawans had to save the prisoners! Ahsoka hit a button to open the doors on the bottom of the ship, and then she, O-Mer and Jinx jumped to safety. ➔

From the beach, the Padawans watched the slave ship crash.

"Well, I guess we won't be escaping on that ship," said O-Mer.

Suddenly they heard a sound from the crash site. It was a survivor! A creature was just visible in the smoke. It was covered in hair, and it was exceedingly tall.

"What is that?" asked O-Mer with a gasp.

The smoke cleared a little, and Ahsoka gave a little smile.

"It's a Wookiee," she said.

Back in the cave, Jinx and O-Mer sat opposite Ahsoka and the Wookiee. Ahsoka could understand his language, and she had learned that his name was Chewbacca.

"Chewbacca, does anyone even know you were taken?" asked O-Mer.

Chewbacca growled glumly.

"No," translated Ahsoka, "but he says his home world is very close."

"It might as well be Coruscant as far as I'm concerned," said Jinx. "We've got no ship."

Chewbacca howled, annoyed by Jinx's negative attitude.

"He thinks he can contact his home planet if we find a way to transmit a signal," said Ahsoka.

"How would we do that?" Jinx demanded. "Send smoke signals? We don't exactly have a transmitter lying around."

"Chewbacca says he can build a transmitter from the wreckage on the beach," said Ahsoka.

It was worth a try. They returned to the crash site and Jinx and O-Mer kept a lookout while Ahsoka and Chewbacca entered the wreck to collect what they needed. Suddenly, a hover pod appeared overhead and dropped off a Trandoshan called Smug. Jinx and O-Mer hid and saw him take aim at the wreck. He had spotted Chewbacca, and they had to do something before their plan was ruined.

Chewbacca and Ahsoka left the wreck, and Smug had a clear shot at them.

"Time to join the Force, Jedi," he muttered. Just as he pulled the trigger, Jinx grabbed his arm. The shot went wide and Ahsoka and Chewbacca threw themselves to the ground. O-Mer and Jinx sent Smug crashing to the beach below. He turned and raised his knife, but then found himself in the vice-like grip of Chewbacca. They had a prisoner.

It didn't take Chewbacca long to build his transmitter. At first it glowed and seemed to be working, but then it went dark.

"We've got a prisoner," said Jinx. "We should be using him to our advantage while we have a chance. It's clear enough that we cannot rely on that device."

Ahsoka wanted to wait, but O-Mer agreed with Jinx. Their plan was to use the prisoner to trick the enemy into flying one of their pods down. They would then hijack the pod, fly up to their base and take them by surprise. Ahsoka couldn't let them go alone, so she persuaded Chewbacca to help them. Hopefully their luck was about to change.

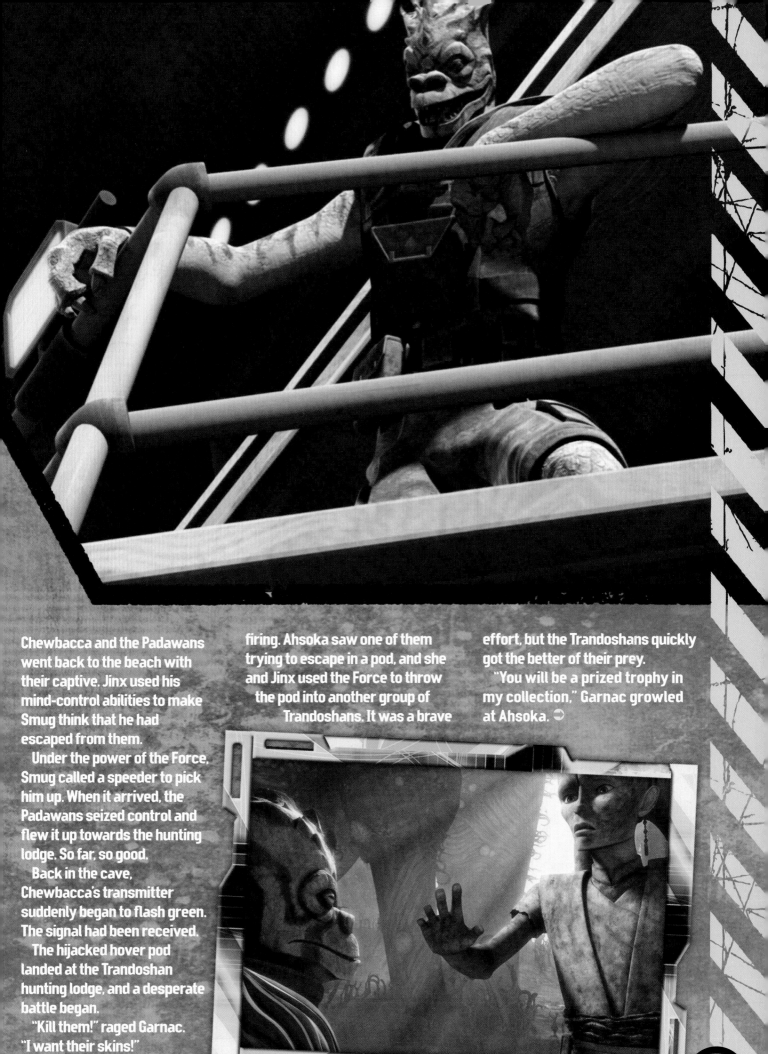

Chewbacca and the Padawans went back to the beach with their captive. Jinx used his mind-control abilities to make Smug think that he had escaped from them.

Under the power of the Force, Smug called a speeder to pick him up. When it arrived, the Padawans seized control and flew it up towards the hunting lodge. So far, so good.

Back in the cave, Chewbacca's transmitter suddenly began to flash green. The signal had been received.

The hijacked hover pod landed at the Trandoshan hunting lodge, and a desperate battle began.

"Kill them!" raged Garnac. "I want their skins!"

The Trandoshans began

firing. Ahsoka saw one of them trying to escape in a pod, and she and Jinx used the Force to throw the pod into another group of Trandoshans. It was a brave

effort, but the Trandoshans quickly got the better of their prey.

"You will be a prized trophy in my collection," Garnac growled at Ahsoka. ➲

Just then, Chewbacca pointed to the sky. A ship was descending towards them, and it was filled with Wookiees under the command of General Tarfful. Chewbacca's signal had worked! The Trandoshans began to fire as the Wookiees charged in.

The Wookiees quickly defeated the Trandoshans, but Ahsoka saw Garnac retreating into the lodge and chased after him. He hurled himself at her, but he had underestimated her skill and strength. After a deadly battle, she used the Force to subdue him.

"You murdered my son and you need to pay for what you did," Garnac scowled.

"Your son died because of your own actions, not mine," said Ahsoka.

Garnac went for his blaster and Ahsoka Force-pushed him out of the door. He fell over the railing to his death.

At last the Padawans arrived back on Coruscant. Mace and Yoda talked to General Tarfful, while the young Jedi were reunited with their masters.

"Ahsoka!" called Anakin, hurrying towards her. "Ahsoka, I am so sorry."

"For what?" she asked.

"For letting you go," said Anakin. "For letting you get taken. It was my fault."

"No, Master, it wasn't your fault," said Ahsoka. "You already did everything you could, everything you had to do. When I was out there, alone, all I had was your training and the lessons you taught me. And because of you I did survive, and not only that, I was able to lead others to survive as well."

Anakin gazed at her with deep respect.

"I don't know what to say," he said.

"I do," his Padawan replied. "Thank you, Master."

She gave him a small bow and he bowed back. And as they walked away together, Yoda watched them with a smile on his face

THE END

71

SPOT THE DIFFERENCE

There are ten differences between these pictures of R2-D2 and C-3PO. Can you locate them all?

AHSOKA

THE NAME GAME

REX

ANAKIN

Which names are hiding in these anagrams?
Unscramble the words and discover the characters.

ARC TROOPER

YODA

1. Pine level

2. Think awful fir

3. Sick oboes

4. Can rag

COOY

5. Lone rat

obi-wan

6. Madmen dry coco

CLONE WARS

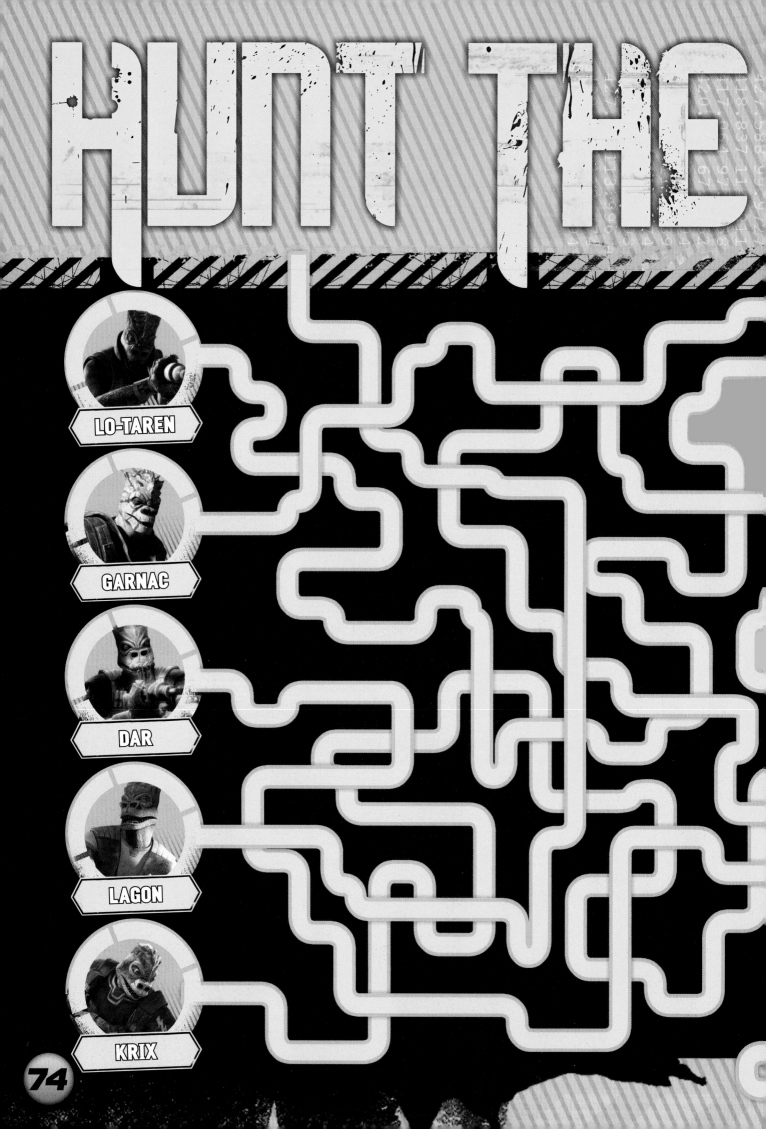

HUNT THE

LO-TAREN

GARNAC

DAR

LAGON

KRIX

HUNTER

Which Trandoshan has caught a Wookiee? Follow the lines with your finger to work it out.

?

CLONE WARS

Trandoshan Trail

Help the younglings to escape the hunters by finding them a safe route through the maze.

START

FINISH

WOOKIEE MUDDLE

ANSWERS

1.
a. Trandoshan b. Wookiee
c. Togruta d. Human
2.
a. Droideka b. Battle droid
c. Astromech droid
d. Medical droid e. Spider droid
f. Crab droid
3.
a. Anakin Skywalker
b. Obi-Wan Kenobi
c. Plo Koon d. Even Piell
4.
a. Bantha b. Neebray
c. Zillo Beast d. Can-cell

Page 12

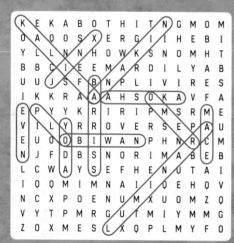

Pages 14-15

Plo Koon, Yoda, Mace Windu
and Even Piell.

Page 24

PYTHON
PIRANHA
TARANTULA
ALLIGATOR
TIGER
EAGLE
BEAR
MAMBA
SHARK
OWL
LION
WOLF
FOX

Page 25

Odd One Out is L

Page 36

1. Ahsoka Tano
2. Anakin Skywalker
3. Plo Koon 4. Luminara Unduli
5. Ki-Adi-Mundi 6. Obi-Wan Kenobi
7. Even Piell 8. Mace Windu

Page 37

The wise leader is Yoda.

Page 48

8	9	5	3	1	7	6	4	2
2	6	7	5	4	8	3	9	1
3	4	1	6	2	9	8	7	5
4	5	8	9	7	3	1	2	6
1	7	2	8	6	4	9	5	3
6	3	9	1	5	2	4	8	7
9	2	3	7	8	6	5	1	4
5	8	4	2	3	1	7	6	9
7	1	6	4	9	5	2	3	8

Page 49

SLEEP
1. BLEEP
2. BLEED
3. BREED
4. BREAD
5. DREAD
DREAM

78
CLONE WARS